Magic
Animal Friends

For Jonah Webb,
with love

Special thanks to Valerie Wilding

ISBN 978-0-545-94080-1

Text copyright © 2015 by Working Partners Limited
Illustrations © 2015 Working Partners Limited

Series author: Daisy Meadows

All rights reserved. Published by Scholastic Inc., *Publishers since 1920*, by arrangement with Working Partners Limited. Series created by Working Partners Limited, London.

SCHOLASTIC and associated logos are trademarks and/or registered trademarks of Scholastic Inc. MAGIC ANIMAL FRIENDS is a trademark of Working Partners Limited.

10 9 8 7 6 5 4 3 2 1   16 17 18 19 20

Printed in the U.S.A.   40
First printing 2016

Amelia Sparklepaw's Party Problem

Daisy Meadows

Scholastic Inc.

Shining House

Sunshine Meadow

Blossom Briar

Toadstool Cafe

Goldie's Grotto

Toadstool Glade

Mrs. Taptree's Library

Friendship Tree

Maze

SilverSpring

Buttercup Grove

Lighthouse

Map of Friendship Forest

Ace Air Travel

Windmill

Mr. Cleverfeather's Inventing Shed

Muddlepups' Den

Treasure Tree

Sparkly Falls

Featherbills' Barge

Waterwheel

Entrance to the Caverns

Swamp

Grizelda's Tower

Can you keep a secret? I thought you could!

Then I'll tell you about an enchanted wood.

It lies through the door in the old oak tree,

Let's go there now—just follow me!

We'll find adventure that never ends,

And meet the Magic Animal Friends!

Love,
Goldie the Cat

Story One
Snapdragon Surprise

CHAPTER ONE

A Special Day

Sunshine sparkled on the water gushing from a tap as Lily Hart filled up a yellow drinking bowl.

"Your turn," she said to Jess Forester, her best friend. "We've got lots to fill!"

Jess pushed her blond curls out of her eyes and knelt to fill a purple bowl.

"I can't decide what I like best about summer vacation." She sighed happily. "There's sunshine, being with you all day ... and spending lots of time at Helping Paw!"

Helping Paw Wildlife Hospital was run by Lily's parents in a converted barn at the bottom of their yard. Jess lived with her dad on the other side of the road and came over as often as she could. Both girls adored animals and loved helping to take care of them.

When Lily and Jess had filled up all the drinking bowls, they put them on trays

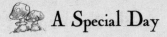

and carried them
to the outdoor pens
and hutches, where
the animals were
all playing in the
sunshine.

Jess put two of
the bowls inside the
guinea pig hutch and rabbit pen. In one
pen, a pair of tiny brown baby bunnies
were hopping around happily. "Aren't
their wrinkly noses cute?" she said.

In another hutch, a tortoise with
a bandaged leg was nibbling on a

dandelion. Lily sprinkled the leaves with water. "You need lots to drink on sunny days," she said. Next, she placed a shallow bowl beside an elderly hedgehog, while Jess went to a pen where a fluffy fox cub lay dozing inside a little den.

"You look a little better today," Jess said, as the fox's ears pricked up. "Here's a drink to keep you nice and cool."

Lily smiled. "This weather reminds me of Friendship

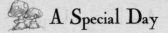

Forest," she said. "It's almost always summer there."

Jess grinned back at her. Friendship Forest was a secret world where something amazing happened—all the animals talked! Some of them lived in little cottages nestled among tree roots, some lived on boats, and others lived in tiny tree houses. Lily and Jess were friends with them all!

"I wonder when we'll see Goldie again," Jess said.

Goldie was Lily and Jess's special friend, a beautiful cat who magically took the girls into Friendship Forest.

As Jess spoke, a flash of gold caught her eye. It was a cat, running through a patch of sunlight. A golden cat . . .

"There she is now! It's Goldie!" Lily said in delight.

The cat bounded over and purred as they stroked her. Then she darted to the bottom of Lily's yard and over the stepping stones across Brightley Stream. Goldie looked back and mewed.

Jess grinned with excitement. "She wants to take us back to Friendship Forest!" she cried. "Come on!"

The girls ran after Goldie and into a
meadow where an oak tree with bare
branches stood. The Friendship Tree! As
Goldie darted up to the tree, it burst into
life. Leaves sprang from the branches and
uncurled, as green as crisp lettuce. Golden
blossoms bloomed and in the grass

beneath,
dozens of
little yellow flowers
appeared. Bumblebees
buzzed and butterflies
fluttered as
goldfinches
swooped
down
to sing
among the
branches.

"Wow," breathed Lily as familiar letters appeared in the tree trunk.

Lily squeezed Jess's hand as together they read the words out loud. "Friendship Forest!"

Instantly, a little door with a pretty leaf-shaped handle appeared in the trunk.

With a thrill of excitement, Jess opened the door. Golden light shone out. Goldie rubbed against the girls' legs, then bounded inside.

Jess grinned at Lily, then they ducked their heads and followed Goldie through the door. Their skin tingled all over, like tiny bubbles were bursting around them, and they knew they were shrinking.

As the light faded, Lily and Jess found themselves standing in a sunlit forest glade, surrounded by tall trees and bushes covered with pink rosebuds. Giant sunflowers bowed over a tiny cottage nestling in the roots of a nearby tree, and bluebirds fluttered in the warm breeze.

"Friendship Forest," said Lily with a sigh of happiness. "Isn't it wonderful to be back at last?"

"I'm so glad you are," said a soft voice.

They turned. Goldie was now standing upright, wearing her golden scarf. She ran

 18

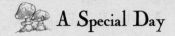

to them and took their hands between
her paws. As the girls were smaller, she
reached almost to their shoulders—and
now that they were in the forest, she
could talk!

A worrying thought struck Jess. "Do
you need our help again, Goldie? Is
Grizelda causing more trouble?"

Grizelda was a horrible witch. She wanted to make all the animals leave Friendship Forest so she could have it all for herself. So far, the girls and Goldie had managed to stop her evil plans.

"Oh, no one has seen Grizelda for a while," Goldie said, smiling. "There's another reason why I've brought you here today—and it's very important."

"What is it?" asked Jess.

"Today is my birthday!" said Goldie. "And I want to celebrate with you, my special friends!"

CHAPTER TWO

The Sparklepaws Arrive

"Happy birthday!" the girls cried, hugging the purring cat.

"We'd love to celebrate with you," added Jess.

Goldie's green eyes gleamed with happiness. "I'm so glad! You're both

invited to my party," she said.
"Lots of our animal friends will
be coming."

"That sounds great!" said Lily.

"I wish we'd known it was your
birthday," Lily said, as they set off through
the forest. "We'd have brought a present."

"Having you here
is the perfect
present!" Goldie
said happily.

Soon they reached a cave
with a red front door with a G-shaped
window—Goldie's grotto! Long strands
of cherry blossom were looped in the
trees, and cushions and chairs were set
outside in the sunshine, ready for guests.
A bunch of balloons hung above the door.

"It looks amazing!" said Jess.

Goldie grinned. "I'm glad you like
it! But the best part is inside.

Mr. Cleverfeather lent me one of his inventions for the party. Come and see!"

Inside, Goldie showed the girls a large machine with a funnel on top and a blue bowl beneath.

"What is it?" asked Jess.

"It's the Dreamy Creamy Ice Machine," Goldie explained. "You fill the top with ice crystals from the Winter Cave. Then you turn the wheel and it makes delicious ice cream!"

"Wow! What flavor?" asked Lily.

"Any flavor you like," said Goldie with a smile. "You can add strawberries

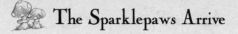

or hazelnuts or whatever you want. Here, let's try cherry flavor." She dropped a pawful of glossy red cherries into the funnel, then said, "Lily, pour that jugful of ice crystals in, too."

Lily did, then Jess turned the wheel. After a few seconds, pink ice cream swirled into the bowl.

"Try it," said Goldie.

Jess and Lily took a spoonful each. It was deliciously sweet and juicy and cold and creamy, all at once.

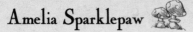

"Mmmm." Lily sighed.

The three friends were tucking into another spoonful when a voice called, "Hello! Is anyone home? We've come to see the birthday cat!"

The girls and Goldie hurried outside. A family of fluffy white cats were coming through the trees—a mom and three kittens.

"It's the Sparklepaws!" Goldie cried.

"Happy birthday, Goldie!" the white cats cried as they hugged her.

"This is Mrs. Sparklepaw and her children, Tommy, Timmy, and Amelia,"

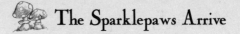

Goldie said, and introduced Jess and Lily.

Amelia was a pretty kitten with shining blue eyes and fur as white as soft, fresh snow. Like her brothers, she was wearing a blue flower on a ribbon around her neck. She bounced over to Goldie and gave her a present wrapped in leaf paper. "It's for you!" she cried. "Open it! Open it!"

"Thank you, Amelia," said Goldie, unwrapping the gift. Inside was a flower filled with perfume.

"I made it myself with flowers from Garland Green, the field behind our cottage," said Amelia proudly. "I used rose petals, violet dew, crushed honeyberries, and a bit of mint."

Goldie dabbed a little perfume behind her ears. "Mmm, it smells just like a summer afternoon," she said, giving Amelia a hug. "Thank you!"

"Look," said Jess excitedly, "all the other guests are arriving!"

Molly Twinkletail the mouse came out of the trees with her nine brothers and sisters. Among them, they were carrying

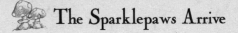

a necklace made of hazelnuts for Goldie.
The Muddlepup dog family arrived, all
four of them carrying pots of jam made

from the berries in their garden, and a
cloud of butterflies, led by the girls' friends
Hermia and Flitta, holding lacy leaves
shaped like parasols. They had brought
birthday cards from animals who lived
too far away to come to the party.

"Thank you, everyone!" said Goldie.

With a flutter of brown feathers, Mr. Cleverfeather the owl landed in front of the grotto. "I've brought you a present too, Goldie—my latest invention. Bappy hirthday! I mean, happy birthday!" He handed Goldie a bowl with a button on one side marked "Blitz." "It's a blender," he explained. "It makes smoothies."

"Thank you!" Goldie said happily.

"Let's try it!" said Amelia, purring with delight.

Goldie took the blender to the bowl of fruit salad on the table outside. Lily was

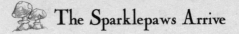

spooning fruit into it when a strange blue furry creature, even smaller than Amelia, scampered on all fours from beneath a starflower bush.

It wasn't like any animal Jess and Lily had seen before. The creature climbed a table leg, grabbed a pawful of berries from Lily's spoon, and scuttled back toward the bush.

Lily dropped the spoon, startled. "Who was that?" she said.

"I'll ask him!" cried Amelia. She bounded after the creature, pounced at his long fluffy tail—and missed. The creature

disappeared back into the starflower bush.

Jess nudged aside the leaves of the bush—then gave a gasp. "Oh! Look!"

On the other side of the bush was a large bouquet of flowers, tied with a big red ribbon.

"Someone must have left them here for Goldie!" said Lily. "I wonder why they didn't give them to her themselves?"

"It must be a birthday surprise!" Jess said with a grin.

CHAPTER THREE
Trapped!

The bouquet was almost as tall as the girls. The gray flowers were like hooked beaks and the stems were covered in mean-looking prickles.

Lily frowned. "It's not a very *pretty* bouquet, is it? There are so many gorgeous flowers in Friendship Forest—

why would someone choose these?"

Amelia sniffed. "Urgh! And they smell like dirty puddle water," she said, her whiskers quivering.

Jess reached out and touched the nearest flower, then drew her hand back sharply. The gray petals felt rough and stiff and horrible.

"Look!" cried Amelia. She pointed a paw at a small envelope tucked into the bouquet. "There's a note!"

The kitten stretched up on her paw-tips and pulled it out. *Goldie,* the envelope said in scratchy writing.

 34

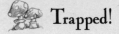

"Goldie!" Amelia called. "You've got some flowers!"

Goldie came hurrying over. "I've never seen flowers like these before," she said curiously. "I wonder who they could be from. Will you open the envelope, Amelia?"

Amelia tore it open and pulled out a card. The girls and Goldie bent over the little kitten to read it. In the same scratchy writing, it said:

Dear Goldie,

Wishing you a HORRIBLE birthday!

From Grizelda

Goldie gave a cry of shock.

"That's awful!" cried Lily.

"Trust Grizelda to try to spoil your birthday," said Jess. "She's always so mean!"

As she spoke, the bouquet rustled. The flowers began to grow, twisting and turning in the air.

Goldie, Amelia, and the girls stepped back, staring in surprise as the beaky flowers grew bigger and bigger.

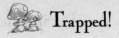

There were shocked cries from behind the girls, where the other party guests were watching.

"They're opening," cried Lily. The flowers gaped wide, looking like big, hungry mouths!

"Keep back!" yelled Goldie.

She and the girls stepped hurriedly away from the flowers—but Amelia was too scared to move!

"Amelia, get back!" Jess cried.

"Look out!" shouted little Tommy Sparklepaw.

But it was too

late. The biggest parrot-beak flower dived toward Amelia.

The kitten gave a squeal as the beak opened even wider, then snapped shut around her.

"She's trapped!" cried Lily.

"My little kitten!" wailed Mrs. Sparklepaw.

Bravely, Jess ran and grabbed the flower. She tried to pry it open, but another flower snapped at her hands. "Ow!" she cried, jumping out of the way just in time.

Lily went as near as she dared and called, "Amelia, are you all right?"

There was a muffled reply. "Y-y-yes!

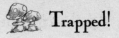

I'm OK. But I want to get out!"

"We'll set you free," called Lily. "And you can have lots of ice cream when we do!"

A flower snapped at Lily, and she darted back to the others.

Mrs. Muddlepup gasped in horror. "Those are snapdragons," she said. "We're always checking to make sure those horrible things aren't growing in our garden. They're impossible to open!"

Lily held Goldie's paw. "Oh, poor Amelia!" she said.

Goldie was in tears. "It's my fault," she

 39

said. "I should be the one trapped inside that flower, not Amelia."

Lily hugged her. "It's Grizelda's fault, not yours," she said. "We'll rescue Amelia somehow."

The horrified animals huddled together.

"I'm scared!" squeaked Molly Twinkletail the mouse.

"How can we save Amelia?" cried Lucy Longwhiskers.

A purple butterfly fluttered over. "I've got an idea," Hermia said in her tinkling voice. She held up a tiny parcel made from a leaf. "There's a drop of sugarsap

 40

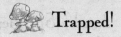

inside," she explained. "We butterflies always carry some to sprinkle on flowers that won't open. It might work with this flower, too."

Hermia flew to the flower where Amelia was trapped. She darted from side to side, so the snapping flowers couldn't catch her, and opened the leaf parcel. A drop of pink liquid fell onto the flower.

Lily, Jess, and the other animals watched

hopefully. The snapdragon opened a tiny bit. Everyone held their breath. But then it snapped shut again.

"Oh, no!" cried Timmy Sparklepaw. "It didn't work!"

Hermia fluttered away from the snapdragons. "We've got more sugarsap in Butterfly Bowery," she said. "If we bring back lots of it, maybe it'll be enough to open the snapdragon."

"We've got to try it," agreed Jess. "It's the only plan we've got to rescue Amelia!"

CHAPTER FOUR

The Butterfly Bowery

Lily, Jess, and Goldie hurried through the forest, following the rainbow cloud of fluttering butterflies. At last, Hermia pointed her wing up into the branches of a willow tree. "There's the Butterfly Bowery," she said. "It's where all the forest butterflies sleep."

Lily, Jess, and Goldie peered up at a little hollow high in the trunk.

"Thanks, Hermia," said Jess. "We'll climb up and get some sugarsap."

"Wait," said Lily. "Even though we're smaller in Friendship Forest, we'll still never fit in that hollow."

Hermia gave a tinkly laugh.

"You will," she said. "Just you wait and see!"

She fluttered alongside them as Goldie led

the way up, bounding

lightly from branch to branch.

The girls followed carefully, and

soon sat beside the cat outside the

Butterfly Bowery. When Lily

peered inside, she gasped at

the sight of so many dazzling,

shimmering butterfly wings.

A yellow butterfly with polka

dots on her wings and an

orange butterfly

with white hearts on hers flew out of the Bowery, carrying tiny purple flowers. They gave them to Goldie and the girls.

"They smell delicious!" said Jess.

"These are shrinking violets," Hermia explained. "If you eat some you'll be able to come inside!"

Lily, Jess, and Goldie each nibbled on a violet. Suddenly, they tingled all over.

"It's like the feeling we get when we

 46

enter the Friendship Tree," cried Lily.
"We're shrinking again!"

"Wow!" gasped Jess. Soon the girls and
Goldie were kitten-sized, and still they
kept shrinking. "I don't think we need
any more!" Jess said, putting the last few
flowers in her pocket. At last, the tingling
stopped.

"We're as small as Hermia!" said Lily—
then laughed. Her voice was as tinkly as
the butterfly's, too.

"Come in!" said Hermia. Now that
they were tiny they could see her clearly.
Her wings were like sails and covered in

swirling patterns of pink,
purple, and lilac.
They followed Hermia
inside. The bowery seemed huge,
with a high ceiling as tall as a cathe-
dral, soft rose petals on the floor, and
a sweet smell in the air. And
everywhere the girls looked
there were fluttering
butterflies of every
color of the

rainbow! Sunlight glittered

through windows covered with

lacy spiderwebs and glinted off the

butterflies' shimmering wings as they

flew around.

"Amazing!" breathed Jess.

"Hello, girls! Hello, Goldie!" said

the butterflies, as Hermia led them to

a pink pool in the ground.

"This is where we keep our

sugarsap," Hermia said.

She showed them

how to dip an empty seed pod into the pool, fill it with sugarsap, then pour it onto a large leaf and fold it into a parcel. Soon Goldie and the girls had made a huge pile of sugarsap parcels.

"I hope we've collected enough to free Amelia," said Jess.

"Me, too," said Hermia. She gave them a handful of sunshine-yellow flowers.

"These are growberry blossoms," the butterfly said. "If you eat them when you get outside, you'll return back to your normal size."

"Thank you, Hermia!" said Lily and

50

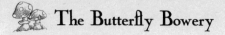

Jess together. The butterflies fluttered their wings in farewell as the girls and Goldie left. On the branch outside, they ate the growberry blossoms. Instantly, they quivered all over and, in no time, they were back to the size they'd been when they arrived in the forest.

"Let's get back to the grotto," said

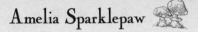

Goldie. "I just hope the sugarsap opens that horrible flower this time!"

At the grotto, the worried animals stood around the snapdragons. The one that held Amelia drooped heavily toward the ground.

"It's all right, Amelia!" Jess called. "We're

going to save you!"

The kitten's voice was muffled. "Please hurry," they heard her say. "It's really dark in here!"

Lily, Jess, and Goldie unwrapped the leaf parcels. Then the girls darted around the flowers, sprinkling the liquid over them as they dodged their snapping petals. When they'd finished, everyone waited. The girls held their breath.

Then the bouquet gave itself a great shake. The sugarsap droplets flew off.

There was a wail from inside the flower. "I'm dizzy!" mewed Amelia.

Finally, the bouquet was still—but the flower holding the kitten was still snapped firmly shut.

Lily and Jess groaned with dismay.

"The sugarsap didn't work!" cried Mrs. Sparklepaw with a sob.

"We're so sorry," Lily said.

She glanced at Jess and Goldie. Their worried faces showed they were all thinking the same thing.

Would they ever be able to free Amelia?

CHAPTER FIVE

An Unwelcome Guest

Nobody knew what to do. The
Sparklepaws huddled together, looking
upset. Mr. Cleverfeather flapped his wings
anxiously and the Twinkletail mouse
family was in tears.

Then Jess gave a shout. She took the
leftover shrinking violets from her pocket

and held them up. "Hey, I know! We can
use these!"

Lily was confused. "How will it help
Amelia if we shrink?"

"We won't eat them," explained Jess.
"We'll feed them to the snapdragons.
They'll shrink until they're too small to
hold Amelia—and then they'll have to
drop her."

"Let's try it!" Lily cried.

Jess crept toward the bouquet,
clutching the violets. As soon as she was
within reach, the flowers snapped at her.
She dodged them, not wanting to get

 56

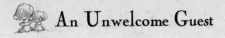

trapped in a flower, too.

Lily shrieked as a flower lunged with its parrot-beak wide open, but Jess was too quick. She tossed the shrinking violets deep inside the flower's mouth.

The flower clamped shut.

Everyone waited.

"Nothing's happening!" Mrs. Sparklepaw wailed.

"Wait!" Goldie grabbed the girls' hands. They watched anxiously as the flowers started to shudder and shake—and then shrink!

"It's working!" Lily cried as the

bouquet got smaller and smaller.

With a slurp, the flower opened, and out tumbled Amelia!

Lily darted forward to catch her, then Mrs. Sparklepaw rushed over to give Amelia a big squeeze.

Everyone cheered. "Hooray!"

The Sparklepaws hugged and kissed Amelia, then she wriggled free and

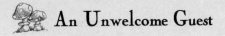

bounded over to Goldie and the girls.

"Thanks for rescuing me!" she said. As she hugged them, the girls could feel her purring.

"You were a very brave kitten," said Lily, stroking Amelia's soft white fur.

"Everything's all right now," Jess said happily. "The party can begin!"

But Lily gave a shout, pointing to a gap in the trees.

A familiar yellow-green orb of light was hurtling toward them!

"Quick, into my grotto!" Goldie shouted, but it was too late.

The orb burst in a shower of smelly green sparks. When they cleared, there stood Grizelda, wearing her usual purple tunic, skinny black pants, and high-heeled boots.

"Go away, Grizelda!" cried Jess. "We've had enough of your evil spells!"

The witch's face was red with rage, and her green hair swished around like tangled snakes.

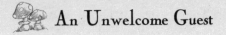

"You've stopped me this time, cat!" she shrieked. "But you won't interfere with my plans again! Ever!"

She snapped her fingers and disappeared in a burst of vile-smelling green sparks.

Lily and Jess turned to Goldie.

"Don't worry," said Lily. "If Grizelda comes back, we'll be ready for her."

"Whatever happens," said Jess. "Now, it's your birthday, and we're not going to let that awful witch spoil your party!"

"No way!" Amelia added bravely.

Mrs. Sparklepaw knelt to hug her kitten

again. "Are you sure you don't want to go home, Amelia?" she asked.

But Amelia shook her head. "I love parties, Mom! I want to stay!"

Goldie smiled at the little kitten. "I'll go inside and start the Dreamy Creamy Ice Machine!"

When she'd gone in, Jess pulled out the little sketchbook and pencil she always carried in her pocket. "Lily," she whispered. "We don't have a present, but at least we can make Goldie a card."

Amelia collected flower petals to decorate the card, and Lily found some

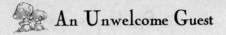

tiny glossy red seeds that she stuck to the card with dabs of sticky pine sap.

They went inside to give the card to Goldie, but the ice cream machine stood silent in the empty cave. Goldie was nowhere to be seen.

"Goldie?" Jess called.

"Maybe she took ice cream out to the others," said Amelia. "I'll look." She scampered away.

"Goldie?" Jess called again.

Amelia came back in, shaking her head. "She's not outside, and no one's seen her," she said. Her whiskers twitched with

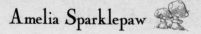

worry. "Where could she be?"

Lily gave a cry of horror. "Oh, no," she said. "Remember what Grizelda said—that Goldie wouldn't stop her plans again? I think she's taken her!"

Amelia gave a frightened mew. "Poor Goldie!"

Jess clenched her fists. "Whatever Grizelda's done with Goldie, we'll find out somehow. We won't let that witch cat-nap our friend!"

Story Two
Cat-napped!

CHAPTER ONE

Where's Goldie?

Lily and Jess sat in despair on Goldie's sofa, with Amelia Sparklepaw the kitten snuggled between them.

Grizelda the witch had already spoiled Goldie's birthday party with one horrible surprise. But now she had done something even worse. She'd cat-napped Goldie!

All the guests were still outside in the sunshine, enjoying the party food. They had no idea that the witch was up to her terrible tricks again.

Lily sighed. "Grizelda told us Goldie would never interfere with her plans ever again," she said. "Where could she have taken her?"

"I keep hoping Goldie's playing touch-a-tail, like I do with my brothers," said Amelia sadly. "That would mean she's just hiding. But she's really gone."

Jess took Amelia's soft little paw. "Come on, let's tell the others what happened."

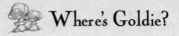

When the animals heard the news, they all gasped in shock.

"Poor Goldie!" squeaked Molly Twinkletail tearfully. "She must be so scared," cried Lucy Longwhiskers, her whiskers drooping.

The butterflies talked worriedly together in tinkling voices, twirling their parasol leaves as they flew.

"And Goldie was so brave helping to get Amelia back," sniffled Mrs. Sparklepaw.

Mr. Cleverfeather hooted mournfully.
"It's a dad bay," he said. "I mean, a bad
day. Where could Goldie be?"

"Maybe Grizelda's taken her to that
terrible witchy tower of hers," Lily
suggested.

Everyone looked around in dismay.
All except Amelia, who was staring at
something on the ground, over where
Grizelda had been
standing. "Look,"
she said. "One of the
butterflies dropped
their parasol leaf."

"Ooh,
yes," said Jess.
"Butterflies," she called,
"has anyone lost their parasol?"

"No," they called in their
tinkly voices.

Lily's eyes shone. "Hey!
If none of the butterflies
dropped the leaf, maybe it
fell from Grizelda's clothes.
It's a clue!"

"You're right!" cried Jess. "If we can find
where it came from, maybe it'll help us
find Goldie. Hermia, where in the forest do

parasol leaves grow?"

"We'll show you," cried the butterfly.

"There's only one parasol tree. Follow us!"

Hermia and her friends fluttered away

in a rainbow swirl.

Lily and Jess started after them, but

Amelia yelled, "I'm coming, too!"

Mrs. Sparklepaw held Amelia's paw.

"Stay here where you're safe," she said.

"Please, Mom," Amelia begged. "Goldie

helped rescue me, remember?"

"Jess and I will take care of her," Lily

said to Mrs. Sparklepaw. "We promise."

"All right," Mrs. Sparklepaw agreed.

Amelia scampered along beside Jess and Lily as they followed the butterflies. Behind them, the animals called, "Good luck!"

"Don't worry," Jess called, "we'll be back soon—with Goldie, too!"

CHAPTER TWO

Amelia's Flower

The butterflies swirled in a colorful, fluttering cloud through the forest.

"Almost there," Hermia said.

Soon they reached the Treasure Tree. Its branches were covered in enough fruit, nuts, and berries for all the animals in the forest. The lower branches were

 75

heavy with golden pineapples. Nearby, the Paddlefoot beaver family was filling baskets with the spiky yellow fruit.

"Hello, Jess and Lily," little Betsy Paddlefoot called. "We're having pineapple pudding today. Would you like to come and have some?"

"We'd love to, Betsy," said Jess, "but we're busy following a clue. It's very important!"

The cloud of butterflies led them on through the trees. Finally, they reached an umbrella-shaped tree.

"The parasol tree!" Lily said excitedly.

The butterflies swirled around it so fast that they made a ribbon of color.

"Thank you, butterflies!" said Jess.

Hermia and her friends called good-bye and fluttered away.

Amelia bounded over to the tree, and the girls joined her to look up through the delicate branches.

"There's no one there," Jess said. "No Goldie, no Grizelda."

Amelia's whiskers drooped.

Jess stroked the kitten's fluffy head.
"We'll keep looking," she promised.

Lily glanced around and noticed
something odd close by. "Look! There's a
strange bush," she told the others.

"Let's take a look," said Jess.

"Be careful," Lily said, picking
Amelia up. She hugged the kitten close.
"Something about it gives me the shivers."

As they drew nearer, they saw it was a
building made of thick, thorny branches
twisted together.

"It's like a huge upside-down nest," Lily

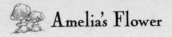

said curiously.

"A really *awful* nest," added Jess excitedly. "It's exactly the sort of place where Grizelda would hide Goldie!"

Lily nodded. "But how will we get inside? There's no door."

"If there's a way in," said Amelia, "I'll find it." She jumped to the ground then crouched low, wriggling forward stealthily on her belly.

The girls tiptoed after her around the outside of the strange building. Whenever Amelia found a space between the branches, she popped her head inside, then moved on to the next gap.

"What are you doing?" whispered Jess.

"I'm checking how wide the gaps are with my whiskers," Amelia explained. She stopped. "Look! Here's a nice big gap!"

Amelia started to scramble through. Lily and Jess crawled on all fours after the kitten, into the thick mesh of thorny branches. Plump, fuzzy-skinned fruit hung from them.

 80

"They look delicious," Jess said.

"Don't touch them," warned Amelia.
"They—"

Just then, Lily's sleeve caught on a thorn.
She jerked back, knocking one of the
fuzzy fruits to the ground.

Screeeeeeech!

The girls covered their ears.

"I was just going to tell you," Amelia
said, "those are screechy peaches! Poppy
and Patch Muddlepup brought them to a
picnic once as a joke. Every time someone
touched them, they screeched! It was
really funny!"

 81

"Grizelda must have put the screechy peaches here so she'd know if someone breaks in," Jess realized.

The screech died away, and was replaced by another sound—the *click, clack, click, clack, click* of the witch's high-heeled boots!

"Who's there?" Grizelda's voice bawled. Her footsteps came closer. "If someone's in my workshop, they'll be sorry. . . ."

"Oh, no!" whispered Lily. "Grizelda's going to see us!"

But Amelia touched the flower around her neck. "She won't," the kitten said. "We can use this!"

"But how can that help?" Jess whispered.

"It's a hiding hollyhock," Amelia explained quickly. "Tommy, Timmy, and I use them to hide whenever we play touch-a-tail. Now hold my paws!"

The frightened girls did as she said. Amelia jangled her flower. Immediately, their hands disappeared—then their arms!

Lily gasped. "We're vanishing!"

"The hiding hollyhock makes us invisible," Amelia whispered.

They froze as Grizelda came closer.

"Someone's in my nice new workshop," she muttered. "I can smell them."

Jess and Lily gripped Amelia's paws tightly as Grizelda's bony nose poked through the mesh of branches. Their hearts were pounding. Would the flower's magic work—or would the witch find them after all?

CHAPTER THREE

Grizelda's Gobbler

Jess and Lily held their breath as they waited. Grizelda pressed even closer against the branches—so close that the girls could have reached out and touched her! Her mean eyes darted all around as she searched.

"Humph," Grizelda said finally. "Must

 85

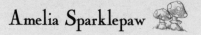

have been a false alarm."

She turned and, to Lily and Jess's relief, her heels started *click-clacking* away as she walked down the hallway.

"She's gone," Amelia said shakily. As she spoke, Lily saw her whiskers reappearing.

"Amelia!" Lily gasped. "You're becoming visible again."

"'Fast and strong, doesn't last long,'" Amelia chanted. "That's what Mom always says about hollyhock magic."

Moments later, they were all completely visible. The girls and Amelia clambered

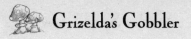

the rest of the way into the workshop
and emerged into a curving hallway, also
made from woven branches. There were
dark wooden doors lining the wall.

Amelia was clinging anxiously on to
Jess's leg. Jess knelt and pet the kitten's fur.
"Amelia," she said gently. "Would you like
to go back home?"

"No!" Amelia said firmly. "Not until we rescue Goldie!"

They went on together to the first door. Jess grasped the handle. "Goldie could be in here," she said, opening it carefully. But the room was empty.

Lily opened the next one, but jumped back in fright when she saw big pots of snapdragons. She closed the door again quickly. Jess eased another door open just enough to

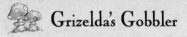

allow her to peep in. She turned to the others, eyes wide, and put a finger to her lips. Silently, she mouthed, "Grizelda!"

Grizelda was crouched down with her back to them, muttering quietly. Bottles of murky-looking liquids and jars of weird objects stood on shelves, and a stack of rusty cauldrons tottered in the corner.

Jess closed the door silently and whispered to the others. "We've got to find out if Goldie is here. Amelia, can you make us invisible again?"

Amelia jangled her hiding hollyhock and took their hands in her paws. Once

 89

they were invisible, Lily opened the door

and they crept inside. Both girls could feel

their hearts racing as they stepped closer

and closer to the witch.

They tiptoed around Grizelda and

saw that she was muttering to the fluffy

blue creature they'd seen outside Goldie's

grotto. He sat on the floor in front of

Grizelda as she fed him

with leaves and twigs.

"There, Gobbler,

you like those,

don't you?" she said. "I'm glad I found you wandering outside my tower. You're exactly what I need to help me take over the forest!"

Gobbler swallowed and gazed up at her with his huge blue-green eyes. "Eeeep!" he squeaked. "Eep, eep, eeeeeeep!"

"You want more to eat, don't you?" said Grizelda as Gobbler munched greedily. Grizelda laughed. "You'll soon have as much as you want!"

She stood, holding a glass jar up to the light. Inside it was a tuft of fur. The strands were gleaming and golden ...

It was all Jess and Lily could do to stop themselves from gasping out loud.

Inside the jar was some of Goldie's fur!

Grizelda made a mark on a piece of parchment that lay beside her. She tucked the jar into her pocket and patted Gobbler roughly on the head.

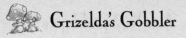

Lily noticed that his blue fur stood on end as the witch touched him. *Maybe he doesn't like Grizelda,* she thought. *Maybe he just likes the food she gives him.*

"Ha ha, little Gobbler!" cackled Grizelda. "I just need to collect one more ingredient and I'll be ready to make my new potion. Then Friendship Forest will be mine!"

Jess, Lily, and Amelia crept out of the room. As they became visible again, they stared at one another in horror.

"So that's why Grizelda kidnapped Goldie," said Jess. "She needed some of her

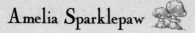

fur to make a potion!"

"I wonder what the potion's for?" said Lily as she cuddled the trembling Amelia.

"It can't be anything good," said Jess. "Whatever Grizelda has planned, we've got to stop her!"

CHAPTER FOUR

Tricking the Witch

"We've got to find Goldie," said Jess, "and we've got to stop Grizelda from finding that last ingredient. Then she won't be able to make her potion."

"But how can we?" Lily said gloomily. "We don't know what the ingredient is."

Amelia was stroking her whiskers

thoughtfully. "I know!" she said. "If we turn invisible again, we can get close enough to read Grizelda's list."

Lily shook her head. "It's too risky," she said. "We were lucky Grizelda didn't hear us before—or bump into us. If only she would leave the room . . ."

Jess grinned. "Screechy peaches!" she said. "Lily, you hide near the door, while Amelia and I make one of the peaches screech. Grizelda's sure to come and investigate the noise. Then you can run in and read the list!"

Lily nodded nervously. Then she

crouched behind a stack of
broken broomsticks, while
Jess and Amelia hurried
along the hallway.

"This is far
enough," said
Jess. She held
Amelia's paw
as the kitten
jangled her hiding hollyhock. Once they
were invisible, Jess tapped one of the
screechy peaches growing on the wall.

Screeeeeeeech!

"I hope this works," said Amelia.

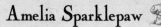

Back by the room, Lily jumped as the door flew open and Grizelda burst out, rushing off in the direction of the noise. Gobbler scampered after her.

Lily's heart raced as she dashed inside. She unrolled the parchment and desperately read Grizelda's scratchy writing. The only ingredient that wasn't crossed off was something called a shower flower.

The noise of the screechy peach was dying

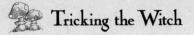

away, so she darted back out, just in time. Grizelda and Gobbler were already coming back down the hallway.

Lily hid until the witch was safely in the room, then ran to Jess and Amelia, who were becoming visible again.

"Did you find out what the last ingredient was?" asked Jess.

"Yes, it's a shower flower, whatever that is," Lily said. "Do you know where they grow, Amelia?"

The kitten shook her fluffy head. "I've never heard of them. Maybe the Muddlepups have them in their garden?"

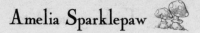

They followed the hallway, away from Grizelda's room.

"We have to stop Grizelda from getting that ingredient," said Jess.

"And we have to find Goldie!" said Lily.

Suddenly, Amelia stopped outside a door. She sniffed, her whiskers twitching.

"I can smell something ... Rose petals, violet dew, honeyberries, and mint ... it's the perfume I gave Goldie for her birthday!" she cried.

Amelia pushed open the door and dashed inside. Lily and Jess darted after her. Inside, her paws tied up with thick

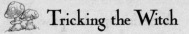

green vines, was Goldie!

"I knew you'd come,"
Goldie cried. "You're so
brave. And Amelia, too!"

"I'm so glad we've
found you!" said Jess.
"How did Grizelda
catch you?"

"I heard an animal crying in the
forest," Goldie explained. "It sounded hurt,
so I went to find it. But it was just one of
Grizelda's tricks."

"We'll get you out," promised Jess.

The girls tried to undo the vines, but

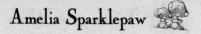

the knots were too tough.

"They won't budge," said Lily. "Grizelda must have used magic to make them extra strong." She heard a pattering sound. "Someone's coming!"

"Grizelda!" whispered Amelia.

"No, her footsteps go *click clack*," Lily said. "It's someone else."

Amelia hid behind her as the footsteps came closer. Then around the bend, padding on his fluffy blue paws, came Gobbler!

CHAPTER FIVE

Rescue

The girls froze, waiting for Gobbler to rush off to Grizelda. But he scampered toward Jess instead.

"Eeeeep!" he squeaked, and started nibbling her shoelaces.

Jess smiled. "He's more interested in eating than helping Grizelda."

Amelia crept out from behind Lily. "He's sort of sweet," she said, "but very greedy!"

Gobbler saw the kitten, and his long tail waved and twirled.

"I think he likes you, Amelia," said Lily.

The kitten padded closer to Gobbler. His tail twirled even more wildly.

"I've got an idea," Amelia said. She patted the thick vines wrapped around Goldie's paws. "Look, Gobbler, these are tastier than shoelaces."

"Eep, eep, eeeeeeeeeep!" Gobbler squeaked. His tail thumped the floor

with excitement.

"Perfect, Amelia!" said Lily. "Gobbler

can chomp Goldie free!"

Jess picked up the wriggly creature so

he could eat the vines around Goldie's

front paws. "Oh," she said. "Amelia, his

fur is almost as soft as

yours!"

Bits of vine fell

from Gobbler's

mouth as

he munched

through

them. He was

halfway through the last one when the girls heard *click, clack, click, clack* . . .

Lily's eyes widened. "Those are definitely Grizelda's footsteps!"

"Run! Hide!" whispered Goldie.

"We're not going without you," Jess said fiercely.

As Gobbler chomped through the last vine, it fell away and Goldie was free!

Clickclackclickclack . . .

"Grizelda's running!" Jess gasped, putting Gobbler down.

"Quick!" Amelia cried. "This way!"

They scrambled through the door and

ran down the thorny hallway, their hearts
pounding.

Clickclackclickclackclickclack . . .

"She's coming!" Lily squealed.

Suddenly, Amelia disappeared.

The friends stopped. "Where is she?"
cried Jess. "Amelia, did you use your
hiding hollyhock?"

But then Amelia's pink nose and white
whiskers appeared in a gap in the wall.
"Through here!" she cried.

Everyone scrambled through to the
outside. With a furious shriek, Grizelda
reached them. But when she tried to

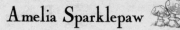

squeeze through the gap, she was too big, and her bony shoulders jammed against the branches.

"Your plan didn't work, Grizelda!" Jess shouted. "We've got Goldie back!" But the witch just cackled.

The girls and Goldie exchanged anxious glances.

"Why is she laughing?" asked Lily. "Her

plan has failed, hasn't it?"

"That cat might have escaped," the witch yelled, "but I've got what I need— her fur! Friendship Forest will be mine! Ha ha haaa!"

"Of course—she means the potion," muttered Jess. "Come on, let's go before she manages to come after us!"

Lily scooped Amelia up and they all raced away from the horrible workshop.

"You were so clever to get Gobbler to help," said Goldie, as they made their way back through the trees to her grotto.

"It was Amelia's idea," said Lily,

cuddling the kitten close.

Jess told Goldie about Grizelda's potion. "We don't know what it is for, but the last ingredient is a shower flower."

Goldie frowned. "I've never heard of a shower flower. Maybe one of the other animals knows what it is."

When they reached Goldie's grotto, they found all their friends sitting gloomily among the decorations. Tommy

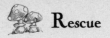

Sparklepaw grinned when he spotted
them, and jumped to his feet. "Look,
they're back! And they've saved Goldie!"
he cried, and the other animals cheered.

Amelia scampered over and hugged her
mom. "I helped!" she told her.

"But Grizelda is still up to something,"
Jess said gravely. "Does anyone know
where shower flowers grow? Grizelda
wants one for a wicked potion."

Everyone shook their heads—even
the Muddlepup dog family, who were
excellent gardeners.

"I've never seen one in our garden," Mr.

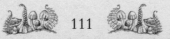

Muddlepup said. "I wish we could help."

Everyone sighed with disappointment.

But then Mrs. Featherbill waved a wing.

"I remember now! I saw one once!"

"Where was it?" Lily asked excitedly.

"You won't find a shower flower today,"

said Mrs. Featherbill. "It's too sunny.

Whenever it rains, the shower flower

grows at the spot where the first raindrop

falls. But it disappears when the sun

shines again."

Goldie looked at the sky. "It'll be dark

soon," she said, "but there are no clouds,

so it won't rain. Grizelda won't find a

shower flower
today, either."

Lily nodded.
"Since it's
almost nighttime,
we should probably go
home now."

Jess grinned. "Or we
could have a sleepover with Goldie and
look for the shower flower tomorrow!
No time passes in our world while we're
away. We can stay and help for as long as
we need to."

"We won't let mean old Grizelda ruin

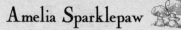

our fun!" Lily cheered.

"Can I go, Mom?" Amelia asked.

"Of course!" Mrs. Sparklepaw agreed.

"Me, too! Me, too!" lots of the other
animals called out.

"Everyone can stay," laughed Goldie.
"It'll be a birthday sleepover!"

Goldie handed out slices of her
birthday cake, while the girls helped
arrange soft piles of cushions and blankets
for the animals to sleep on.

Amelia curled up in the middle with her
brothers, purring contentedly as her eyes
drifted closed.

Once everyone was comfy, the girls
settled beside Goldie and gave her the
card they'd made before her party started.

"Oh, thank you! It's the nicest card
I've ever gotten," Goldie told them. She
smiled happily. "Grizelda tried to ruin my
birthday, but it's still been very special—

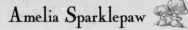

because you're here, Lily and Jess."

There was a sleepy mew. "And me," purred Amelia.

Everyone laughed!

"Especially you!" said Goldie.

She turned to Jess and Lily and whispered, "All I need now is to stop Grizelda from ruining our forest—then I'll be the happiest cat ever!"

Story Three
Greedy Gobbler

CHAPTER ONE

Mr. Cleverfeather's Inventing Shed

Lily and Jess woke up in a nest of blankets and cushions in Goldie's grotto. Morning sunshine streamed through the G-shaped window in the door and shone on the sleeping animals curled up all around them.

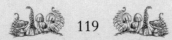

Jess stretched her arms and sat up. "I'm so glad we found Goldie," she said, whispering so she wouldn't wake the others.

"But we still have to stop Grizelda," Lily said seriously.

The witch had kidnapped Goldie from her own birthday party. The girls and Amelia Sparklepaw, their kitten friend, had rescued her, but Grizelda was now planning to make a potion. Lily and Jess didn't know what the potion was for, but they knew it would be something horrible!

Goldie and Amelia stretched and yawned. Then they curled up again, so close that

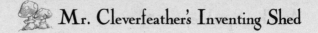

their whiskers were touching.

"Wakey wakey!" said Jess, gently shaking them. "We have to stop Grizelda from finding a shower flower and completing her potion, remember?"

Amelia's blue eyes flew open. "Ooh, yes," she said eagerly.

Goldie got up. "Don't worry. We've beaten Grizelda before. We'll do it again."

As all of the animals started to wake up, Goldie opened the door and sunlight flooded in. The girls looked outside.

"Oh, dear. It won't rain today," said Lily.

"It might," said Jess. She pointed up at

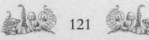

some gray clouds floating high above the trees. "Hopefully a shower flower will grow somewhere!"

Goldie made everyone a breakfast of toasted sunflower seed buns and whipped up banana and honey smoothies in the blender Mr. Cleverfeather had given her for her birthday. While they ate, Goldie said, "If a shower flower does grow today, how can we find it before Grizelda does?"

"I know!" said Lily, looking at the blender. "Let's ask Mr. Cleverfeather if he has an invention that can help."

Mr. Cleverfeather the owl hadn't stayed

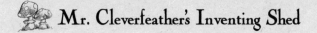

for the sleepover, so after saying good-bye to everyone, the girls, Goldie, and Amelia set off to his tree. Lily and Jess watched the sky anxiously.

Goldie pressed the trunk of Mr. Cleverfeather's tree with her paw. The rough surface rippled and twisted, and a winding staircase appeared.

Amelia's eyes widened. "Wow!"

Lily and Jess grinned. The girls had seen Mr. Cleverfeather's home before, but they still found it amazing!

Amelia scampered up the stairs and the girls and Goldie followed. At the

top was a
shed, with Mr.
Cleverfeather standing
in the open doorway.
He was wearing his usual
waistcoat and monocle
and hooted happily when
he saw them.

"Come in!" he said.
"How can I help you?"
Once he'd heard what
the problem was, he
rummaged through his
inventions. Soon he

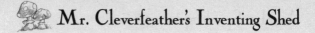

tossed out an object with a propeller and a basket hanging underneath.

"Hovering Apple-Picker—that never worked," he muttered. "What's this?"

A set of wheels with a board fixed on top rolled out. "Hmm, that surfboard was supposed to work on sand and lea," he said. "I mean, land and sea. But it sinks."

Then, hooting with glee, he produced a contraption kind of like a watering can. He pressed a button and a red-and-blue-striped umbrella shot out of the top.

"My Dropper Spotter!" said Mr. Cleverfeather. "It detects drainrops—

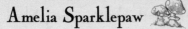

I mean, raindrops.
It's useful when you're
planning a picnic."

Goldie, Amelia, and
the girls cheered.

"Hooray!" said Lily. "Now we can find
the exact place where the shower flower
will grow."

Jess picked up the Dropper Spotter. "I
just hope we find it before Grizelda does.
If she manages to make her potion, I'm
sure something terrible will happen to
Friendship Forest . . ."

CHAPTER TWO

The Dropper Spotter

"You just bess that prutton," Mr. Cleverfeather explained to Jess. "I mean, press that button. Then off you go!"

"Thanks, Mr. Cleverfeather!" said Jess.

They waved good-bye to the owl and went back down the magical staircase.

Jess put the Dropper Spotter on the
ground and pressed the start button.

The umbrella began to turn. Soon it
was spinning so fast that the red and
blue stripes became a blur of purple. The
Dropper Spotter rose until it was level
with Jess's head, and took off through the
forest, zooming around the trees.

Lily picked Amelia up, and they all
hurried after it.

As they pushed
through the bushes, the
kitten's ears twitched and
she gave a sudden cry.

"Stop! There's someone calling nearby!"

They waited a moment, watching the
Dropper Spotter anxiously in case it flew
out of sight.

"Oh! I can't hear anything now ..."
said Amelia.

"Maybe it was the wind blowing in the
bushes," Lily suggested.

"Yes," said Amelia. "Maybe."

They hurried on. When the Dropper Spotter whizzed around a group of nut trees, Amelia stopped and put a paw to her ear.

"There it is again!" she said. "I can definitely hear a voice—it came from behind those jellyberry bushes!"

Jess and Goldie followed her to investigate. Lily jumped up and grabbed

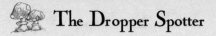

the Dropper Spotter so it wouldn't get too far ahead, then joined them.

But there was no one behind the bushes.

"That's funny." Amelia scratched her head in surprise.

"Help!" a voice cried. "Please help me!"

"I heard it, too!" cried Jess. "It's coming from that bush with orange flowers . . ."

As Lily, Jess, and Amelia ran over to the bush, Goldie shouted after them, her tail twitching with worry.

"No, wait!" the cat yelled. "That's how Grizelda kidnapped me, remember—she used a spell so I thought an animal was in trouble! It's a trap!"

But it was too late. There was a sudden explosion of stinky sparks in front of the girls and Amelia. Standing with Gobbler tucked under her arm was Grizelda!

CHAPTER THREE

Shower Flower

With a triumphant cry, Grizelda snatched
the Dropper Spotter from Lily. "Ha
haaa!" she cackled. "I knew you'd fall for
it if I called for help. Serves you right! You
just can't keep your noses out, can you?"

She pressed the Dropper Spotter's start
button and the umbrella started to turn.

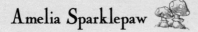

"Ha haa!" she crowed. "Now I'll find the shower flower!"

"Eeeep!" squeaked Gobbler as the witch dashed after the Dropper Spotter.

The four friends set off at top speed behind her.

"Hurry!" Goldie cried as she ran. "She's getting away."

Grizelda looked around, laughing as sparks flashed from her high-heeled boots.

"She's using magic to go faster," Lily groaned. "We'll never catch up."

"Keep going," yelled Jess. Amelia was panting for breath, so she scooped

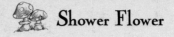

the kitten up. "Grizelda will stop if the

Dropper Spotter does!"

"Run!" cried Goldie, glancing up at the

gray clouds overhead. "The sky's getting

darker. It will rain soon."

They raced on until they came to a

large clearing near the parasol tree.

"Look!" Lily cried, pointing. "There's Grizelda. And Gobbler! The Dropper Spotter's stopped!"

"That must be where the first raindrop will land," said Jess.

As she spoke, the sky darkened. A gray cloud loomed overhead, right above where Grizelda was standing.

Goldie, Amelia, and the girls watched in horror as a single raindrop fell from the cloud, glittering like a diamond. The drop fell lower and lower until it splashed onto the dry ground at Grizelda's feet.

Instantly, a green shoot sprang up,

glistening with the raindrop's moisture.

The rain started falling harder and, as
it did, the shoot began to grow. When it
was as tall as Grizelda, a huge blue flower
burst into bloom.

Lily gasped. "The shower flower!" she
cried. "Quick, let's get it!"

They raced toward the tall plant,
but they were too late.
Grizelda's long, bony
fingers reached out
and plucked it.

Cackling with glee,
she pulled a glass flask

from inside her cloak. She crumpled the flower and stuffed it inside. Only then did she look at Goldie and the girls.

Grizelda smiled her cold smile and waved the flask. "You're too late," she said, gloating. "All the ingredients are in here. My potion is complete and there's nothing you can do!"

She shook the flask from side to side.

"Oh, no!" Lily breathed.

Amelia buried her face in her paws. "What's the potion going to do?"

CHAPTER FOUR

Gobbler Grows

Goldie, Amelia, and the girls watched helplessly as Grizelda's flask bubbled and fizzed. Dingy green smoke flowed over the top, leaving a thick liquid behind.

Grizelda poured the liquid onto a handful of leaves and put them on the ground in front of Gobbler.

"Eeeeeep!" he squeaked delightedly and began chomping on them. But after a moment, he had to stretch down to reach the rest of the leaves.

Jess gave a cry of alarm. "So that's what the potion does—he's getting bigger!"

They watched, horrified, as the furry blue creature grew larger. He bounded to a nearby bush and quickly munched his way through it, still growing. His shell-shaped ears grew as big as saucers, and his tail was twice as long as Goldie's.

"He's already much bigger than Amelia," said Goldie, her green eyes wide

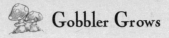

with worry. "How big is he going to get?"

"Big enough to eat up the entire forest!" Grizelda cackled. "That's right, my lovely, eat up!"

Gobbler swallowed the rest of the bush, and his fluffy blue body grew so he was as tall as the girls! Amelia gripped on to Lily's leg, trembling.

"Oh, no!" said Goldie as Gobbler chomped a whole tree branch.

Gobbler stretched up on his hind legs to start eating a holly tree. His tail waved and twirled, swishing around like a gigantic feather boa.

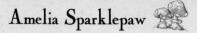

"There has to be a way to stop him!"
cried Lily.

The witch danced in delight. "Oh, no,
there isn't!" she crowed. "Gobbler
will gobble everything—trees,
smelly flowers, the animals'
homes, and their awful
belongings. They'll all
leave. In a few hours,
Friendship Forest
will be mine, all
mine!"

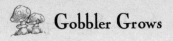

Jess clenched her fists. "You won't win,
Grizelda!" she yelled. "We've beaten you
before and we'll do it again!"

Grizelda ignored her. "Eat up, Gobbler,"
she screeched. "I'm going to my tower to
get my things ready to move here."

She snapped her fingers, and vanished
in a smelly burst of
sparks.

Gobbler
gobbled
on. "Eep,

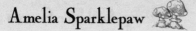

eep," he squeaked, licking his lips with his long red tongue.

Jess groaned with despair. "We'll never stop him. He loves eating too much!"

Amelia and Goldie hugged each other miserably as Gobbler ate everything around him.

"We must do something," said Goldie. "Think hard, everyone!"

Lily had a thought. "What if we got Gobbler to eat Grizelda's workshop?" she said. "Those tough branches would keep him busy, and it would give us time to

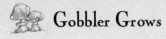

think of a way to break the spell."

"Perfect!" said Jess. "Amelia, Gobbler likes you. Could you persuade him to come with us?"

"I'll try," Amelia said nervously.

She padded forward and called, "Gobbler?"

The creature was twice the size of the girls now. He looked down at Amelia and blinked his big blue-green eyes.

"Come with me, Gobbler!" Amelia called, setting off in the direction of the workshop. "We know where there's lots of delicious food!"

"EEP!" said Gobbler, his voice now loud and booming. "EEEEEEEP!"

He followed after Amelia, his huge paws thumping on the ground. Lily, Jess, and Goldie hurried after them.

"Are you all right, Amelia?" Lily called.

"I think so," the kitten replied over her shoulder. "He's actually really friendly, even though he's so big!"

As soon as they reached the workshop, Gobbler started gnawing through the tough branches. With each mouthful, he swelled up more, and more, and more, until

he towered over the workshop itself.

Goldie sighed with despair. "We'll never be able to feed him enough to stop him from ruining Friendship Forest."

Lily nodded. "I wish we could make him smaller, like we did with the snapdragons."

Amelia tugged on Lily's hand, quivering with excitement. "We can! Let's give him shrinking violets!"

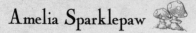

"There aren't any," said Jess. "We used the last ones on the snapdragons."

"I know where we can get some more!" cried Amelia, her blue eyes shining. "Garland Green, where I got the flowers to make Goldie's birthday perfume! We can ask my mom and my brothers to help ... This way!"

They left Gobbler munching on the workshop and followed Amelia to a buttercup-yellow cottage. Outside the front door was a slender plant with a golden flower at its tip. As the group hurried up the path, Amelia jangled

one of the plant's
leaves and the
flower tinkled like a
doorbell.

The door opened
and there stood
Amelia's mom with
Tommy and Timmy. Amelia quickly
explained what they were doing.

"Goodness, you'll need lots of violets
to shrink a creature that size," said Mrs.
Sparklepaw, wringing her paws. "Of
course we'll come and help!"

The girls and Goldie ran after the

Sparklepaws to Garland Green. It was covered in grass and dotted all over with colorful flowers. On one side was a huge patch of shrinking violets, their purple petals quivering in the breeze.

"There they are!" cried Jess. She and Lily ran to pick some. But as they reached down to pick the flowers, the petals shut tight and the flowers disappeared into the ground.

The girls gave cries of dismay.

"Oh, no!" said Lily. "If we can't pick them, then we can't stop Gobbler!"

CHAPTER FIVE

Not the Treasure Tree!

"I don't understand," said Jess, shaking her head. "Hermia managed to pick lots of shrinking violets."

"That's because butterflies are small enough to creep up on them," Amelia explained. "Shrinking violets are really shy. So we'll all need hiding hollyhocks!"

Tommy darted across Garland Green, and came back with a pawful of blue flowers, exactly like the hollyhocks the kittens were wearing. He handed them to his mom, Goldie, and the girls.

"Now jangle them!" said Amelia.

They giggled as they watched one another disappear. When the tip of Goldie's tail had vanished, they tiptoed toward the shrinking violets.

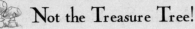

"Sorry, Mom! Sorry, Amelia!" whispered Timmy. "I keep bumping into everyone!"

This time, the flowers stayed up so they could pick them. They worked quickly, and the sight of handfuls of flowers floating in the air made Jess smile. "I think we've got enough," she said after a while. "Now let's just hope they work as well on Gobbler as they did on the snapdragons!"

Gobbler had just finished eating the thorny workshop when they got back.

"Wow!" said Jess. "He's almost as big

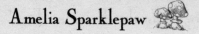

as the Treasure Tree now!"

Amelia tiptoed as near as she dared, calling, "Gobbler! Yummy treat! Come and get it!"

He thudded toward her.

"Hold out the violets!" said Goldie.

Gobbler sniffed the flowers. But then he jerked away. "YUCK!" he spluttered.

He looked over the girls' shoulders, and his eyes widened.

"EEP," he boomed, his tail thudding on the ground, "EEP, EEP . . ."

Everyone turned to see what he was looking at. In the distance was a tall tree

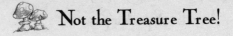

laden with fruit of all kinds.

"The Treasure Tree!" cried Lily. "We have to stop him from eating it. If only he'd eat the shrinking violets . . ."

As Gobbler set off for the Treasure Tree, Jess yelled, "I've got an idea! I just need one of the butterflies to deliver a note . . ."

She pulled out her sketchbook and pencil and scribbled a message. Then she made a butterfly shape with her hands, just as Goldie had once shown them, and fluttered them like wings.

Moments later, Hermia fluttered down. Jess gave her the note. "Please take

this to Mr. Cleverfeather, as quickly as possible," she said.

"On my way!" Hermia said in her tinkling voice, and flew off.

The four friends followed Gobbler, trying to slow him down with snacks of cones and leaves.

As they neared the Treasure Tree, Jess froze. "Oh, no! Look!"

A familiar yellow-green orb was floating toward them.

It burst into sparks, revealing Grizelda with a wide grin on her bony face.

"My plan's working," she cackled. "Eat up, Gobbler!"

Goldie and Amelia began frantically searching for tasty things to tempt Gobbler away from the Treasure Tree. Jess whispered to Lily, "Gather up leaves and twigs for when Mr. Cleverfeather arrives."

Just then, they heard a soft hoot, and Mr. Cleverfeather appeared overhead, wearing a harness with whirring blades fixed to the back.

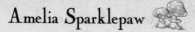

"He's turned himself into a helicopter!" said Jess.

Lily nodded. "And he's brought the blender with him!"

"I asked him to get it from Goldie's grotto," explained Jess. "I just hope my idea works . . ."

Mr. Cleverfeather dropped the blender into her arms. Then he flew around Gobbler's head, hooting. "Treave our lee alone!" he cried. "I mean, leave . . . Oh, you know what I mean!"

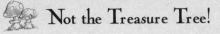

Jess stuffed the violets into the blender, and Lily added twigs and leaves. They blended them into a purple liquid, which trickled into the mug on the side of the blender.

Lily glanced over. Grizelda wasn't watching Gobbler—she was meanly picking fruit off the tree and squashing it under her high-heeled shoes. "Now!" Lily whispered.

"Here, Gobbler!" Jess called. "I've got a delicious drink for you!"

The great furry creature bent his massive head down toward them and

sniffed. "EEEEEEEEP," he thundered,
so loudly the girls flinched, and opened
his mouth.

Jess poured the drink inside.

"SLUUURP," went Gobbler.

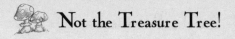

"SLUUUUUUUURP!"

Instantly Gobbler started to change. He looked surprised as he shrank as quickly as a popped balloon. "EEEEEEP!" he squeaked.

The witch turned, staring in disbelief. "Nooooo!" she screeched, stamping her feet angrily.

Gobbler got smaller and smaller, until he was his normal size—even tinier than little Amelia. He sat under a fir tree, crunching cones and squeaking happily.

"He'll never eat the forest now, Grizelda!" said Jess.

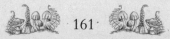

The witch loomed over the girls. "You've won this time!" she shrieked, "but mark my words. Friendship Forest will be mine. One day!" she screamed, shaking her fists. With a snap of her fingers she disappeared in a shower of sparks.

"Eeeeep!" Gobbler said, rolling over to show off his fluffy, round tummy.

"I think he's full at last," said Amelia with a laugh.

The girls and their friends joined hands and paws in a dance of joy.

CHAPTER SIX

One Last Surprise

When Lily, Jess, Goldie, Amelia, and
Gobbler reached Toadstool Glade, it
was eerily silent. Usually animals were
bustling around, or sitting outside the café,
but today there was no one in sight.

"What's wrong?" said Goldie.

Suddenly, animals everywhere burst out

of hiding, shouting, "Surprise!"

Lucy Longwhiskers ran over. "Mr. Cleverfeather told us what you all did. There's a birthday tea waiting at the Toadstool Café, to make up for Goldie's party being ruined!"

"And to celebrate defeating Grizelda!" said Mr. Longwhiskers.

Everyone rushed over as quickly as they could. There were cheese-and-walnut grilled cheeses, honey biscuits, and Dreamy Creamy Ice Cream in lots of flavors.

Gobbler's appetite was back. He waved his tail as he ate a bowl of ice cream.

"He's sweet, isn't he?" Jess said.

"What will happen to him?" Lily asked.

"Mom says he can live with us!" said
Amelia, stroking Gobbler's fluffy head.
"His job will be to eat all the weeds in
Garland Green."

The girls felt happy that Gobbler had
someone to care for him. They hugged
Amelia and stroked her soft fur.

"We have to go home now," Jess
said. "But we'll come and visit you and
Gobbler as soon as we can."

"I'll miss you," Amelia said. "We had a
scary adventure, but it was fun, too."

 166

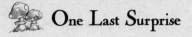

When everyone had said good-bye,
Goldie took the girls to the Friendship
Tree. "Thank
you for rescuing
me and for
saving our
forest," she said.
"I'll never forget
my exciting
birthday!"

Goldie touched a paw to the tree trunk
and the door appeared.

The girls stepped through the doorway
into golden light. When the shimmering

glow faded, they found themselves back in Brightley Meadow.

"What an amazing adventure," said Lily, as they ran back to Helping Paw. "I'm glad Friendship Forest is safe."

"Wasn't it a great party?" said Jess.

Lily nodded. "It was," she said, "but I didn't have any ice cream. I wonder if Mom has some?" She giggled. "I feel like I could eat as much as Gobbler!"

The End

Olivia
Nibblesqueak's
Messy Mischief

by
Daisy Meadows
creator of
Rainbow Magic

SCHOLASTIC

Lily and Jess are needed back in Friendship Forest—when Grizelda and her new helpers cast a spell to make the good animals naughty!

Turn the page for a sneak peek of

Olivia Nibblesqueak's Messy Mischief

Grizelda beckoned to the creatures from the Witchy Waste.

"These are my new helpers," she said. "Don't meddle with them if you know what's good for you."

The bat flapped onto her shoulder.

"This is Peep," said Grizelda, "and here comes Masha."

Masha the rat was wearing a rumpled straw hat with a droopy flower stuck into the band. She coiled her tail around the witch's leg, grinning.

"Snippit!" Grizelda called.

The scruffy crow, whose waistcoat

had a button missing, flew to her other
shoulder.

Grizelda nodded at the slimy toad,
who straightened her necklace and
waddled over. "I'm Hopper," she croaked.

Grizelda laughed. "You girls won't
be able to stop my new helpers. They're
going to make the forest so messy that
all the animals will have to leave. Then
Friendship Forest will be mine!"

She raised her hands. Purple sparks shot
from her fingers and crackled around
each Witchy Waste creature.

Then, with a final cackle, Grizelda

snapped her fingers and disappeared in a burst of smelly yellow sparks.

"Thank goodness she's gone," said Jess.

"What were those purple sparks?" wondered Lily. "Do you think they're one of Grizelda's nasty spells?"

Goldie nodded. Her tail was twitching anxiously.

Now that Grizelda was gone, the animals began to come out from the bakery. Olivia Nibblesqueak was shaking icing from her rose crown.

"Squeeeaak!" Peep the bat flew straight toward her. He flapped his wings over

the little hamster, and the girls gasped as
purple sparks reappeared and crackled
around her.

"Heeheehee," giggled Peep the bat.
"This will be fun!"

Jess looked at Lily in alarm. "Oh, no!
That bat did something to Olivia!" she
said. "But what?"

Read

Olivia Nibblesqueak's Messy Mischief

to find out what happens next!

Visit Friendship Forest, where animals can talk and magic exists!

Meet best friends Jess and Lily and their adorable animal pals in this enchanting series from the creator of Rainbow Magic!

SCHOLASTIC

scholastic.com

MAGICAF2

RAINBOW magic™

Which Magical Fairies Have You Met?

- ❏ The Rainbow Fairies
- ❏ The Weather Fairies
- ❏ The Jewel Fairies
- ❏ The Pet Fairies
- ❏ The Dance Fairies
- ❏ The Music Fairies
- ❏ The Sports Fairies
- ❏ The Party Fairies
- ❏ The Ocean Fairies
- ❏ The Night Fairies
- ❏ The Magical Animal Fairies
- ❏ The Princess Fairies
- ❏ The Superstar Fairies
- ❏ The Fashion Fairies
- ❏ The Sugar & Spice Fairies
- ❏ The Earth Fairies
- ❏ The Magical Crafts Fairies
- ❏ The Baby Animal Rescue Fairies
- ❏ The Fairy Tale Fairies
- ❏ The School Day Fairies

■ SCHOLASTIC

Find all of your favorite fairy friends at
scholastic.com/rainbowmagic

RMFAIRY14

RAINBOW magic™

SPECIAL EDITION

Which Magical Fairies Have You Met?

❏ Joy the Summer Vacation Fairy
❏ Holly the Christmas Fairy
❏ Kylie the Carnival Fairy
❏ Stella the Star Fairy
❏ Shannon the Ocean Fairy
❏ Trixie the Halloween Fairy
❏ Gabriella the Snow Kingdom Fairy
❏ Juliet the Valentine Fairy
❏ Mia the Bridesmaid Fairy
❏ Flora the Dress-Up Fairy
❏ Paige the Christmas Play Fairy
❏ Emma the Easter Fairy
❏ Cara the Camp Fairy
❏ Destiny the Rock Star Fairy
❏ Belle the Birthday Fairy
❏ Olympia the Games Fairy

❏ Selena the Sleepover Fairy
❏ Cheryl the Christmas Tree Fairy
❏ Florence the Friendship Fairy
❏ Lindsay the Luck Fairy
❏ Brianna the Tooth Fairy
❏ Autumn the Falling Leaves Fairy
❏ Keira the Movie Star Fairy
❏ Addison the April Fool's Day Fairy
❏ Bailey the Babysitter Fairy
❏ Natalie the Christmas Stocking Fairy
❏ Lila and Myla the Twins Fairies
❏ Chelsea the Congratulations Fairy
❏ Carly the School Fairy
❏ Angelica the Angel Fairy
❏ Blossom the Flower Girl Fairy
❏ Skyler the Fireworks Fairy

■SCHOLASTIC

Find all of your favorite fairy friends at
scholastic.com/rainbowmagic

3 stories in each one!

HiT entertainment

RMSPECIAL18